RANGO

A HERO AT LAST

By
ANNIE AUERBACH

Based on the screenplay written by
JOHN LOGAN

Story by
**JOHN LOGAN,
GORE VERBINSKI,**
and **JAMES WARD BYRKIT**

STERLING

New York / London
www.sterlingpublishing.com/kids

STERLING and the distinctive Sterling logo are registered trademarks of
Sterling Publishing Co., Inc.

Library of Congress Cataloging-in-Publication Data Available

Lot #:
2   4   6   8   10   9   7   5   3   1
12/10
Published by Sterling Publishing Co., Inc.
387 Park Avenue South, New York, NY 10016

Distributed in Canada by Sterling Publishing
C/o Canadian Manda Group, 165 Dufferin Street
Toronto, Ontario, Canada M6K 3H6
Distributed in the United Kingdom by GMC Distribution Services
Castle Place, 166 High Street, Lewes, East Sussex, England BN7 1XU
Distributed in Australia by Capricorn Link (Australia) Pty. Ltd.
P.O. Box 704, Windsor, NSW 2756, Australia

Sterling ISBN 978-1-4027-8444-6

For information about custom editions, special sales, premium and
corporate purchases, please contact Sterling Special Sales
Department at 800-805-5489 or specialsales@sterlingpublishing.com.

Rango was lost in the desert.

He was tired. He was hot.

He needed some water.

FAST!

Rango walked and walked.

Finally he found a town called Dirt.

It was full of cowboys.

He tried to act like a cowboy, too.

Rango walked into a saloon.

Everyone turned to look at him.

They didn't like strangers.

"Where are you from?" asked a mouse

named Spoons.

Rango replied, "I'm not from around

these parts. I'm from the West.

The Far West."

"Who are you?" Spoons asked.

"My name is Rango," he said.

Elbows the cat had a question.

"Are you the fellow that got rid of the

Jenkins brothers?" he asked.

"That's right," said Rango.

Everyone gasped.

Rango knew he told a lie.

But he wanted to fit in.

Just then the doors slammed open.

It was Bad Bill and his gang!

Everyone was scared of them.

They were mean. They were nasty.

And they were UGLY!

Bad Bill saw someone new in the saloon.

"That there is Rango," said Spoons.

"He's not afraid of you."

"Is that right?" asked Bill.

Rango gulped. Things were bad.

Then they got worse.

Bad Bill challenged Rango to a

showdown!

Bad Bill and his gang stood at one end

of Main Street.

Rango stood at the other end.

He was very nervous.

He hoped Bad Bill would change his mind.

Rango tried to stay calm.

He wanted to be tough.

"Now, listen. I'm going to give you

fellows one last chance to reconsider,"

he said.

Suddenly, a big, scary hawk flew above.

Rango did not see it.

Bad Bill looked scared.

Then he ran off!

"Now that is what I'm talking about!"

said Rango.

"Listen up," he called out.

"Rango is in town.

Things are going to be different

around here."

Rango turned around.

The big, scary hawk looked right at him.

Rango's eyes opened wide.

Then he ran!

Rango dashed into the outhouse.

He slammed the door.

That didn't stop the hawk.

The bird sliced the outhouse apart

with his claws.

Rango was scared and ran again.

The hawk followed him.

The townsfolk thought that Rango

was chasing the hawk!

They cheered him on.

The angry bird flapped his wings.

He got closer and closer to Rango.

Rango grabbed onto the water tower.

CRASH! The water tower fell down.

It landed right on the hawk!

The townsfolk walked outside.

They looked at the hawk.

"We can't believe it," they said.

Everyone was excited.

"It's about time we had a hero around

here," said a toad named Waffles.

"Let's hear it for Rango!" said Elbows.

"Yahoo! Yee-haw!" cheered the townsfolk.

"I think it's time he met the mayor,"

said Buford, the bullfrog.

The mayor was up to no good.

But he welcomed Rango anyway.

"I think this town has a bright future,"

he lied.

"I hope you'll be part of it."

The mayor opened a box of sheriff stars.

He picked one up.

He placed it on top of the box.

"Pick it up, Mr. Rango," said the mayor.

"Your destiny awaits."

Rango pinned on the sheriff star.

He was the new sheriff in town.

He was a hero at last!

★ BEHIND THE SCENES ★

The amazing art and life-like animation for *Rango* was not made overnight. It took artists and illustrators months to perfect every last detail of the characters. Before making it to the big screen, the talented team at Industrial Light and Magic created hundreds of character and set sketches, sculptures, and paintings for inspiration and research. Their animation experts then took that hand-drawn artwork and used it as a basis for the final CGI (computer-generated imagery) animation you see in theaters. Here is some "behind-the-scenes" art that shows how *Rango* came to life.

Original sketch of the saloon

Final version of the saloon

Painting of the hawk

Heroic sketch of Rango

Heroic painting of Rango